W9-BYH-284

A FRIBBLE MOUSE LIBRARY MYSTERY

The Secrets of the Sea Chest

Phyllis J. Perry

Illustrations by Ron Lipking

UpstartBooks

Fort Atkinson, Wisconsin

For all of Fribble's fans and especially for Casey, Clare, Julia, Emily, Kenny, and Colleen.

Published by UpstartBooks
W5527 Highway 106
P.O. Box 800
Fort Atkinson, Wisconsin 53538-0800
1-800-448-4887

Copyright © 2007 by Phyllis J. Perry

The paper used in this publication meets the minimum requirements of American National Standard for Information Science — Permanence of Paper for Printed Library Material. ANSI/NISO Z39.48.

All rights reserved. Printed in the United States of America.
The purchase of this book entitles the individual librarian or teacher to reproduce copies for use in the library or classroom. The reproduction of any part for an entire school system or for commercial use is strictly prohibited. No form of this work may be reproduced or transmitted or recorded without written permission from the publisher.

"Fribble!" Mother called. "Would you please get the mail? I just saw the postman walk by. Bring it to me here in the kitchen, and then you and Scamper can come have a snack. I've taken the first batch of cookies out of the oven."

As soon as he heard his mother call, Fribble Mouse leaped up and put down the crossword puzzle he'd been working on. He needed no more urging. Fribble had already sneaked his paw into the delicious cookie dough earlier. For the past several minutes his mouth had been watering as he smelled the wonderful aroma of baking peanut butter cookies floating in from the kitchen. He loved them almost as much as he loved cheese. Fribble's little brother, Scamper, who had been lying on his stomach on the carpet in the living room, immediately dropped the book he was reading and raced for the kitchen. He was a peanut butter cookie fan, too.

Fribble hurried out into the bright Saturday afternoon sunlight, opened the mailbox, and scooped up a pile of letters in his paws. He scampered back into the house and dropped the letters at one end of the kitchen table. Mother had already placed a plate of cookies in the middle of the table and was pouring two glasses of cold milk while Scamper happily nibbled away. Fribble slid into a chair and reached for a warm cookie, eager to catch up with his little brother. While Fribble munched and crunched, he watched as his mother opened a long envelope and started to read.

"Well, that is news," she said.

"What?" Fribble asked.

"Your Great Uncle Skipper Mouse is moving. He's tired of keeping up the big house and yard and he's selling or giving away most of his furniture. Imagine that! He'll move into a little cottage in September. I didn't know he was planning to leave that wonderful old house he lives in."

"I don't remember any Great Uncle Skipper," Scamper said. "Who is he?"

Mother smiled. "You've never met him, dear. He lives quite a long ways off, near the Atlantic Ocean, in a town called Edam, Maine."

"Near the ocean? Wow! I've always wanted to see the ocean," Scamper said.

"Have I met him?" asked Fribble.

4

"Yes," his mother said, "but you were only a tiny baby mouse. Great Uncle Skipper was here in Cheddarville, Wisconsin, visiting some old friends the very week you were born. He came over to see you. My! You were squeaking and making a terrible fuss when he got here! Great Uncle Skipper insisted on taking you in his arms, and he rocked you until you fell fast asleep."

"Really?" Fribble said.

"Really. You know your great-uncle is called Skipper Mouse because he was a sailor," Mother explained. "And he said the reason you went right to sleep when he held you was because you were a born sailor, too, and liked to be rocked as if you were on the ocean waves."

Fribble smiled. He wished he could remember his Great Uncle Skipper. He sounded awfully nice.

"Didn't he ever come back and visit again?" Scamper asked.

"No. He's very old, and he doesn't travel much anymore."

Fribble and Scamper both reached for a second cookie. At the same time, Mother went back to reading her letter.

"Well, well. More news," she said after a moment. "It seems that Great Uncle Skipper remembered you, Fribble, after all this time. Listen to what he wrote." Mother cleared her throat and read out loud, "'I am mailing my old sea chest to little

Fribble, who I've always known was a real sailor mouse at heart. It's not terribly valuable, although I did buy it in China when I sailed there long ago. It's traveled with me on the seven seas and holds a few things that Fribble might find of interest. Be watching for it, because it will be arriving soon.'"

"A sea chest!" Fribble said. "I wonder what's in it and when it'll come?"

"Any day, I suppose," his mother said.

"Boy, are you lucky." Scamper's whiskers drooped. "And Great Uncle Skipper was lucky, too. He got to sail all the way to China, and I've never even seen the ocean once. I wish I could go to the ocean."

"Wait, there's more," Mother said, as she continued reading the letter. She put it down and smiled. "Scamper, you may just get your wish."

"Honest?" Scamper's eyes were shining. "How?"

"Great Uncle Skipper asks if we'd like to come for a visit this summer before he moves out of his big old house. He says he has lots of room, his house is right on the beach, there's a lighthouse close by, and it would be a wonderful summer vacation."

"Wow!" Fribble said. His eyes sparkled at the thought of vacationing at the seashore.

Scamper got so excited, he slid out of his chair, ran to his mother, and grabbed her paws. "Do you

think we can really go?" he begged, as he danced up and down.

"I'll certainly talk to your father about it. Maybe we can," his mother said. Mother gave Scamper a hug.

"And look! There's a note enclosed for you, Fribble." She handed a sheet of paper over to Fribble.

"What does it say?" Scamper demanded.

Fribble read the note aloud. "'Dear Fribble, I'm sending you a sea chest filled with secrets. You'll have to be a good detective to figure out what everything is. Good luck! Love, Great Uncle Skipper.'"

Fribble's eyes were shining. He loved secrets and mysteries. What could be in that old sea chest?

Scamper ran back to his seat, and between bites of his second cookie, started telling his mother about all the things they might do at the seashore. For a little mouse who had never even seen the ocean, he had a lot of ideas.

Fribble sat quietly as he ate the remainder of his cookie, but although his body was still, his long tail was twitching and his mind was racing. What would be in that sea chest? Fribble wished it were here right now. He sighed.

"What's wrong, dear?" Mother asked.

"I wish it was summer already, and we could pack up and go on vacation and see the Atlantic Ocean."

"It'll be summer before you know it," his mother said.

But Fribble knew it was only early May and he faced another whole month of school. After wiping the last cookie crumb from his whiskers, Fribble asked, "Is it all right if I go for a walk to the library? I have some homework I need to do." Fribble knew it was crazy, but somehow he thought if he got started on his final school project it would make summer come faster.

"What sort of homework?" Mother asked.

"It's our last big project of the school year," Fribble explained. "Mrs. Tremble, my teacher, is explaining careers. She's teaming up with Miss Longwhiskers, the librarian; Mr. Fiddler, the music teacher; and Miss Sketch, the art teacher. Our project is called Careers: Past, Present, and Future."

"What are careers?" Scamper asked.

"Careers are the different kinds of jobs that people do," Fribble explained. "I could write about being a gold miner of long ago who struck it rich out West. Or I could write about being a lawyer today, or an astronaut or a robot expert in the future."

"What career will you pick, Fribble?" Scamper asked.

"I don't know yet." Fribble furrowed his brow. "And it's more than reading and writing. Mrs.

Tremble says we need to bring in something special to share."

"Like what?" asked Scamper.

"Last Friday in music class Mr. Fiddler explained that there are lots of interesting songs about what people did in the olden days. 'I've Been Working on the Railroad' tells what it was like to build train tracks across the country. Miss Sketch, the art teacher, says we might find pictures about a career we pick to study, like a drawing of cowboys on a cattle round-up."

"So you have to find some music or pictures to go with your report?" Mother asked.

"Or we can bring in other things, too. Like if I studied being an architect, I could bring in an architect's drawing. Or if I studied a career as a doctor, I might bring in an X-ray."

"Sounds very interesting," Mother said. "You've got lots to think about."

"Yeah," Fribble said. "And I thought I might get some ideas at the library."

"That's a good place to start," Mother said.

"Could I come, too?" Scamper asked.

"Sure," Fribble said.

Mother glanced at the clock. "Be sure to be home by five o'clock. Take Scamper's paw when you cross a street, Fribble, and be careful to look both ways."

"Okay," Fribble agreed. "I'll go get my notebook."

Fribble ran to his room to pick up his spiral notebook and a pencil. Then he rushed back to the kitchen to get Scamper. "Come on," he said. But before he headed for the door, he walked over to the kitchen table and took one more cookie. "Energy food," he explained to his mother. "Thanks for baking them. They're really good!"

Scamper quickly grabbed another cookie, too.

They left the house and started down the street, nibbling as they went. The library was only a few blocks away, and Fribble and Scamper had been there many times. As soon as they reached it, they hurried up the steps and inside.

In the children's section, Miss Scurry, the librarian, greeted them. They were such regular visitors that she knew them by name. "Good afternoon, Fribble and Scamper. I'm glad to see you. Could I help you find anything special today?"

"He's investigating careers," Scamper said, obviously proud of his new word.

"Careers? What sorts of careers?" asked Miss Scurry.

"I don't know," Fribble said. "I need to find a really good career to study."

"Hmmm," Miss Scurry said. "Sounds like the first thing you need to do is narrow your search a little.

Maybe the computer card catalog would be a good place to start. You could read the names of some of the career books we have, and maybe something will sound especially interesting."

While she talked, the three of them walked over to an open computer.

"Where do I start?" Fribble asked.

"Remember that you'd like to look at books written for young readers," Miss Scurry said. "So what word do you need to type in?"

"Juvenile," Fribble said promptly. "That'll give me books that kids can read."

"Right. Try typing in 'careers' and 'juvenile' and see what you get."

Another child was waiting for help by her desk, so Miss Scurry said, "I'll come back in a few minutes and see how you're doing."

Fribble typed in "careers juvenile," and as he watched in astonishment at how many titles immediately appeared on the computer screen, his little heart beat faster. Maybe one of them would be the career for him!

"Wow," Scamper said as he stared at the computer screen in the library. "There are lots and lots of careers, aren't there? And some of those words are awfully hard. Will you read them to me?"

"Yes," Fribble agreed, "there are a lot of careers." He looked at the list of book titles, and, as he skimmed the list, he read them aloud to Scamper. "There's actor, ballerina, doctor, filmmaker, firefighter, musician, police officer, secret service agent ..."

"Stop!" Scamper said. He held up his paw. "Secret service agent would be cool, wouldn't it? Why don't you pick it for your career? And for your special stuff you could bring in a coded message or a paw print or something."

Fribble smiled. His little brother did have good ideas. But as he turned back to the long list of careers showing on the computer screen, he sighed.

"What's the matter?" Scamper asked. "Wouldn't you like to be a secret service agent?"

Fribble sighed again. "It's hopeless," he said.

Just then Miss Scurry came walking up. "What's hopeless?"

"There's too much to choose from," Fribble said. "It's like being in an ice cream shop with a huge list of flavors and trying to pick out just one. They all sound really good, but which one should I pick?"

"You're probably going to spend a lot of time on your project," Miss Scurry said, "so you should choose something you're really interested in learning more about. Is there some special job that you think you'd like to do yourself some day?"

"I keep changing my mind," Fribble said. "One day I think I want to be an artist, but the next day, I think I'd like to be a baseball player. Then I want to be a detective. That's the problem. I like lots of different things."

"That's not a problem. That's good," Miss Scurry said. "You've got many, many years to decide what you might want to do. Even after you think you know, you may still change your mind several times."

"So if I don't really know what I want to be when I grow up, what career should I pick for my report?"

"Maybe you'd like to know more about the work of someone in your family, someone who you think has had a very interesting career," Miss Scurry suggested.

Fribble looked at Scamper, and Scamper looked back at him. They both grinned and said at the same time, "Great Uncle Skipper!"

Miss Scurry smiled. "And what does your Great Uncle Skipper do?"

Fribble puffed up proudly. "He was a sailor. He lives in Maine by the Atlantic Ocean near a light-house, and he's sailed the seven seas."

Miss Scurry smiled. "There you are! You've picked your career."

"A sailor," Fribble said. "Just like Great Uncle Skipper."

"I think you'll have fun finding out about sailors and the sea, Fribble." Miss Scurry said. "Long ago, there were big clipper ships that sailed in the China trade. And there were people who went to sea to harpoon whales. Some people today join the Navy or the Coast Guard or dive in submarines. And besides sailors, there are lots of other sea-related jobs. You could investigate some of those, too. People used to be lighthouse keepers. Some dive for sunken trea-sure. You might study the work of a marine biologist. There are lots of careers to explore."

"Wow!" Fribble said. "It'll be fun to read and write about the sea."

"Do you think you want to read about a career from the past, the present, or the future?" Miss Scurry asked. "Once you decide that, you can find a

lot of information from books and magazines, and maybe ask your great uncle some questions, too."

"I think I want to study a sea career from the past," Fribble said, "and I can hardly wait to get started."

Fribble thought that studying about the sea would be a fun way to end the school year. With an excited twitch of his tail, he also realized he'd learn a lot of stuff that would help him get ready to enjoy a summer vacation with Great Uncle Skipper, too, if they got to go to Maine. Maybe he'd even read about old sea chests and what was in them.

"Okay, we need to find books about the sea," Scamper said. He smiled at his big brother as he slid off his chair and looked at all the shelves filled with hundreds and hundreds of books. Slowly the smile faded and was replaced by a look of bewilderment. "There are lots and lots of books in here, Fribble. How do you know where to start looking?"

"I'm going to start right here at the computer catalog," Fribble said, as he thoughtfully stroked his long whiskers. "I'll enter some words into the computer and we'll find out what books this library has. I'll copy down the names and numbers and that'll tell us where to look for the books on the shelves."

Miss Scurry nodded on hearing this. "Good idea. You know how to use the library, Fribble. If you need help, just let me know."

Miss Scurry left, and Fribble turned back to the computer. This time he typed in "sailor" and "juvenile." He started to browse through the titles that came up on the computer screen.

"Do any of them look good?" Scamper asked. He had climbed back onto his chair and was peering over Fribble's shoulder.

"Yeah," Fribble said. "Here's one that's called *The Sailor Through History*. That might tell me something about sailing in olden times. Its number is 910.45." Fribble wrote down the title and number in his notebook.

"Let's go look for it," Scamper said, starting to climb off his chair again.

"Not yet. I'll find some more possibilities first. Then we can go and hunt for all of them at once."

Fribble turned to face the computer screen again. "Hey! Look at this," he said, pointing to the screen as his long tail began twitching. "This book is called *Sailor Song*."

"Oooh!" Scamper said. "Do you think there'll be a song in it that you can share with the class as one of your something specials?"

"Maybe," Fribble agreed.

"What's its number?" Scamper asked.

"It doesn't have a number," Fribble explained. "It's a picture book. Picture books are kept in a special part of the library. They're put on the shelf in alphabetical order by the author's name. Nancy Jewell wrote this book so I'll look for it in the 'Js' for Jewell in the picture book section."

"Now do we go look?" Scamper asked again, one paw already touching the carpet.

"Not yet," Fribble said, smiling at his eager little brother. "Don't be in such a rush. Hold your sea horses!"

That made Scamper giggle.

"Here's another interesting one," Fribble said. "It's called *John Paul Jones, America's Sailor.* I think I'd like to read that. Its number is 973.35092 Jones."

"Okay, that's three books we have to look for." Scamper looked hopefully at his brother, but he stayed in his chair.

"Yeah, but I'm still not finished. I think I'd like to look at a book about lighthouses, too. Remember, Great Uncle Skipper said there was a lighthouse near where he lived. We might be seeing it this summer. Lighthouses sound really cool."

Fribble typed "lighthouse" and "juvenile" into the computer and waited. "Here's one. It's called *The Lighthouse Book* and its number is 387.155." Fribble wrote this into his notebook, too. Fribble would have liked to look up sea chests, but he didn't think his little brother could stand to wait much longer. "Now, Scamper, it's time to look for books."

Scamper leaped off his chair, ready for action.

Fribble led the way first to the picture books where they found *Sailor Song*. Then they went to the nonfiction stacks where they tracked down two more of the books that they wanted. Fribble couldn't locate the third book on his list, so he led the way to Miss Scurry's desk.

"Find everything you were looking for?" she asked.

"I couldn't find this one about John Paul Jones," Fribble said. "Maybe it's already checked out."

"What's its name and number?" Miss Scurry asked.

Fribble turned to the page in his notebook where he'd written *John Paul Jones, America's Sailor* and 973.35092 Jones.

Miss Scurry typed the information into her computer. "It should be on the shelf," she said. "Did you look in the biographies? We keep those in a special section. They're not listed under the author's name, but are shelved alphabetically by the name of the person that the book is about."

"So I have to look in the biographies under 'J' for Jones?"

"That's right, Fribble." Miss Scurry led the way to a set of shelves filled with biographies. Fribble found the book about John Paul Jones, and they headed back toward the checkout desk.

"You've found some good books to get you started," Miss Scurry said. "Anything else you need now?"

Scamper spoke up. "We may be going on a vacation to see the ocean," he said. "Is there a good book for me?" He hesitated and then he added, "It has to be pretty easy 'cause I can't read big words yet."

"Of course there's a good book for you," Miss Scurry said. She took a detour over to the picture book section. "Let me check to see if one of my favorites is in." She quickly found what she was looking for. "Here it is," she said, pulling a book from the shelf and handing it to Scamper. "Does it look good to you?"

Scamper looked at the cover. It was *The Ocean Alphabet Book*. Then he opened it up. "Help me read the first page, Fribble," he said.

Fribble read the first page. "'A is for Atlantic Ocean. The fish and other creatures in this book live in the North Atlantic Ocean.'"

"That's the ocean next to where Great Uncle Skipper lives, isn't it?" Scamper asked in great excitement.

"That's right, Scamper," Fribble said.

"Then this is the book for me," Scamper said, and he clutched it tightly.

Fribble and Scamper headed home from the library. It was a beautiful spring afternoon. Fruit trees bloomed, and tulips brightened several gardens. The scent of lilacs filled the air. But Fribble didn't stop to sniff the air or admire yards. He was eager to get to his house and start reading.

When Father Mouse arrived home for dinner, everyone began talking at once and pleading for a vacation at the seashore to visit Great Uncle Skipper. Father wasn't hard to convince. He was as excited as the rest of them.

"It sounds like a great idea," he said. "I'll phone Uncle Skipper to see what dates work best for him. Then I'll check my calendar at the office on Monday and find out when I can take my two-week vacation."

"Yay!" Scamper cheered, as he danced up and down. "We're going to the ocean! We're going to the Atlantic Ocean!"

Fribble managed not to dance up and down, but he stroked his whiskers all the way to their tips, and his tail flicked from side to side in excitement as he thought of the fun they were going to have.

All weekend there was a lot of sea talk at Fribble's house. Whenever he could find someone to listen, Scamper would show a page from his ocean book and talk about the sharp teeth of a bluefish or explain about the many arms of an octopus.

At breakfast, lunch, and dinner, no matter how a conversation started out, Fribble somehow quickly turned it back to the sea. Saturday night, Mother served a basket of biscuits with dinner. "If we were old-time sailors," Fribble said, as he took a warm biscuit and bit into it, "we'd be having hardtack."

"What's that?" Scamper asked.

"I just read about it," Fribble said. "It's a biscuit that sailors and soldiers used to eat. But it wasn't like Mother's biscuits. Hardtack was so hard that you had to smash it or dip it into something to soften it up before you ate it."

"Hardtack doesn't sound too good to me," Scamper said. "Do you think you'll make hardtack and take some to school for one of your something specials?"

"Maybe," Fribble said.

"What are something specials?" Father asked.

Fribble told him how his class was studying careers, past, present, and future, and how he was going to report about sailors.

At Sunday breakfast, as he drank his orange juice, Fribble said, "Old-time sailors used to get sick with scurvy because they didn't have enough fresh fruit to eat."

When he wasn't talking about the sea, Fribble was reading about it. As he kept poring over his library books, Fribble jotted things down in his spiral notebook so he'd have lots of information for his written report.

On Monday morning at school, Fribble told his friend Tweek that he was going to write a report about being an old-time sailor.

"What career are you going to write about?" Fribble asked.

"Music," Tweek said, "either being a composer or pianist."

That didn't surprise Fribble because Tweek played the piano very well. "Good choice," Fribble said. "And it'll be easy for you to find something special. You can play a piece or bring in a recording of music by one of the composers you'll read about. I don't know if I'll have any music to share, or not. I checked out a book called *Sailor Song*, but I don't think I'll use it, 'cuz it turned out to be a baby's lullaby."

Even though he wasn't going to bring in the lullaby for one of his something specials, Fribble liked the song. When he read the book, it made him think about the story his mother told him about Great Uncle Skipper rocking him to sleep as a baby.

"During music today, ask Mr. Fiddler about sea songs," Tweek suggested. "I'll bet he has some ideas."

When Fribble got to music class the last period of the day on Monday, he told Mr. Fiddler that he was going to write his career report about sailors. "Do you know any sea songs?" he asked.

"Of course," Mr. Fiddler said. "There are lots of sea shanties."

"What's a sea shanty?" asked Fribble.

"Shanties are songs that sailors sang while they worked. They'd sing when they pulled up the anchor, or as they pulled ropes to hoist the sails, or while they worked on the pumps. Our library has sea shanties on CD. Check them out and listen to the songs at home. Maybe you'll pick a favorite to share with the class."

When school ended, Fribble gathered his things and hurried to the library. Miss Longwhiskers, the school librarian, was standing behind the checkout counter.

"Hi, Fribble," Miss Longwhiskers said. "What are you hunting for today?"

"Mr. Fiddler said that our library has a CD of sea shanties. I'd like to check it out."

"Come with me," Miss Longwhiskers said. She led him to a small section of the library where CDs and videotapes were housed. "We don't have a lot of CDs, but we do have a great one of sea shanties." She helped him find it and check it out.

"I didn't know we had CDs and videos in our library," Fribble said.

"Well, we don't have many, Fribble," Miss Longwhiskers said. "If you don't find a song here that you like, the public library has more CDs than we do, and you can look there, too."

"Thanks," Fribble said. "For my career report, I'm studying sailors, and I'm hoping I'll find a song that I like to share with the class."

Fribble tucked the CD in his backpack and ran off to meet Scamper, who was waiting for him outside his room so they could walk home from school together.

As soon as they reached home, Fribble and Scamper went straight to the kitchen to have their after-school snack. Mother already had cheese, apple slices, and crackers on the table, and she quickly poured glasses of milk.

Fribble told his mother that he'd checked out a CD of sea songs. "I want to listen to them right away."

"As soon as you finish your snacks," Mother said.

Fribble glanced at his mother as she spoke. Immediately he knew something funny was going on. She was wearing an "I've-got-a-secret sort of smile." But she didn't say anything.

When Fribble finished his snack, he took the CD out of his backpack and raced to the living room to play it, with Scamper right behind him. But he stopped when he saw the big box, sitting right in the middle of the living room floor. All thoughts of the CD flew out of his mind as he stared at the package. It stood almost as tall as Fribble.

"Is that my sea chest?" Fribble asked his mother. "Is it here already?"

"That's it!" Mother said. "A delivery truck brought it just about an hour ago."

"Can I open it?" Fribble asked.

"Of course," Mother said. "I'll go get a knife."

Mother came back with a knife and used it to cut the tape that held the flaps together. When she was finished, she said, "All right! It's ready for you to open!"

Mother sat on the couch while Fribble sat on the floor. Scamper kneeled close to his brother, not wanting to miss a thing.

Inside the box there was bubble wrap, which Fribble pulled out and tossed in all directions to the carpet. Finally, he saw some dark wood.

"I see it!" he shouted. "It's my sea chest."

Fribble stood and leaned over into the big box. He grasped the end of the chest in his paws and pulled, but it was too heavy for him to move.

"I can't get it out," he said as he tried again.

"I'll help." Scamper jumped to his feet and leaned into the box, too. But still the chest would not budge.

"Let me try," Mother said. She came over, reached inside, and got a good grip on both ends of the box, but she couldn't pull the tightly wedged chest out.

Mother picked up the knife that she had put down on the coffee table. "I'll cut the corners of the box," she said. "And don't worry. I'll be very careful not to scratch the chest."

Scamper and Fribble sat close and watched as Mother cut from the top corner to the bottom on all four sides. The sides fell down and there, still covered in a sheet of bubble wrap, was the sea chest. Fribble quickly tore off the last of the wrapping, and all three of them sat admiring it.

The chest was made out of dark teak wood. There were two brown leather straps that went all around it, sort of like belts. The hinges and the lock were made of brass. They were shiny, as if Great Uncle Skipper had polished them before mailing the chest to Fribble. Taped to the top of the chest was an envelope.

Fribble tore open the envelope. Inside was a note and a brass key. The note was from Great Uncle Skipper. The writing was thin and spidery looking. Although Fribble was good at reading printed words, he still found the handwriting hard to read.

"Will you read it out loud, Mother?" Fribble asked.

Mother began to read the letter. "'Dear Fribble, Your mother has told me you like to solve mysteries. Here is my old sea chest. I hope you like it. It holds lots of secrets. You'll find four boxes inside. I've numbered each one. Please open them one box at a time. Be a detective and find out what you can about what each box holds before you open the next one. You'll find lots of surprising things. If you get stuck, phone or write me, and I'll help you out. Love, Great Uncle Skipper.'"

Fribble took the brass key, and, with a shaking paw, inserted it into the lock, where it turned easily. Fribble's eyes were shining, and he held his breath as he opened the lid.

Inside the chest were four boxes, stacked two deep, each about the size of a shoebox. The boxes

were wrapped in plain brown paper and tied with sturdy twine. And each box had a number written on top of it.

"Pirates' treasure chests are always filled with jewels," Scamper said, speaking barely above a whisper. "Are there rubies and diamonds inside those boxes?"

"This isn't a pirate's chest," Fribble explained. "It's Great Uncle Skipper's sea chest that sailed with him on the seven seas. He didn't keep jewels in it. He kept important sailor stuff in it."

"What kind of stuff?" Scamper asked.

"Mysterious stuff," Fribble said. "Stuff I need to investigate and find out about."

Fribble carefully took the box labeled number one from the chest. He sat down on the rug and tugged hard, trying to break the cord tied around it, but it was too sturdy. Mother took the knife again and cut the twine.

Fribble hesitated for just a moment. He stroked his whiskers and his nose twitched. Then he quickly tore away the brown paper and lifted the lid of box number one. Holding his breath, Fribble peeked inside.

There, inside the box in a nest of tissue paper, lay a piece of wood, twice as long as it was wide. The wood had been sanded smooth on both sides and painted a glossy black. Fastened on the wood, one below the other, were six different knots, each tied in narrow white rope. The knots had been glued onto the wood. Also glued on, just beneath each knot, was a small, blank, white tag.

"What's that?" Scamper asked, leaning over Fribble to stare at the piece of wood.

"Sailor knots, I think," Fribble said, as he reached out and gently traced his paw around each twist and turn of one of the knots. His whiskers quivered.

"I didn't know there were so many knots,"

Scamper said. "The one I use to tie my shoelaces is hard enough. Why do you need lots of different knots?"

"I imagine a sailor uses many knots for different jobs on a ship," Mother said.

"Are you going to learn to tie all those knots?" Scamper asked Fribble.

"Maybe," Scamper said, continuing to look at them closely. "At least most of them. Hey, look!" Fribble dropped the knot board. "I think there's something else in this box."

Fribble reached inside and took out a bulky object that was also wrapped in tissue paper. Once unwrapped, Fribble found himself holding something about the size of a plum. It was another knot, a complicated looking one. Narrow white rope went around something in the center from left to right three times and then around again from top to bottom three times. The rope completely covered whatever was in the middle. The ends of the rope hung out from behind it. There was also a little blank, white tag dangling down from it on a string.

"What's that thing?" Scamper asked.

"I don't know," Fribble admitted. He lifted it, feeling its weight. "It's heavy."

Then Fribble noticed a card that was taped inside the cover of the box. He ripped it off, looked at the printed message, and read it out loud. "Can you find out the names of these knots and print them on the tags? Can you learn how to tie them?"

"Of course I can," Fribble answered out loud, just as if Great Uncle Skipper were there in the room and could hear him. Fribble's long tail swished through the air. "I'm going to start investigating and find out the names of all these knots, and then I'm going to practice until I can tie every one of them! And I want to start right away. Mother, can I make a quick trip to the library?"

"Me too?" asked Scamper, scrambling to his feet.

Mother glanced at the clock. "Yes, as long as you're home by five o'clock."

Fribble got his notebook and pencil out of his backpack, and he and his little brother hurried down the street to the library.

In the children's section of the library, Fribble and Scamper saw Miss Scurry helping someone at her desk. She looked up long enough to smile at them.

Fribble led the way to the computer and clicked to open the computer catalog screen. He typed in "knots juvenile." Two titles came up. Fribble clicked on the first title, *Handbook of Knots*, to get more information.

"This book is on the shelf," Fribble said, his whiskers quivering. "That's good. And look! It says 'a step-by-step guide to tying and using more than 100 knots.'"

"Perfect!" Scamper said. "Just what we want."

Fribble copied down the author's name and the number 623.8882. Then he hit the Back button and read the second title that had also come up on the screen, *Knots to Know*. Again he clicked to get more information.

"Hey, this one sounds good, too," Fribble said. "See," he pointed to the screen, it has 'how-to illustrations.'" He read on. "Oh, no! Someone has it checked out."

"Are there any more?" Scamper asked. "You usually look up a lot of titles before we go hunting for them."

"More what?" Miss Scurry asked as she came up to them. She smiled. "What exciting books are you looking for today? Books about sailors and oceans?"

"Books about sailor knots," Fribble said. He told her about the sea chest that had arrived in the mail and the challenge he had of naming and learning to tie the knots. "I guess there's only one knot book on the shelf."

Miss Scurry checked what Fribble had already done in the card catalog. "You're right. But we have more knot books in the adult section of the library. Sometimes young readers need to use adult books, you know. Directions for tying knots can be complicated, but you might find something in the adult nonfiction section that would be helpful."

"How would I find them?" Fribble asked.

"Just type in 'sailor knots' and don't add the word 'juvenile,'" Miss Scurry explained.

Fribble typed in "sailor knots." Immediately, nine book titles appeared on the screen.

"Hey, there are lots more books about knots in the library." Fribble breathed a sigh of relief. "This one is called *The Art of Knots: A Sailor's Handbook.* That sounds good."

Fribble copied down the author's name and the number 623.8882.

"And here's another." Fribble pointed to an entry on the screen. "*Great Knots and How to Tie Them.*" Once again he copied down the author's name and the number 623.8882.

Scamper got a puzzled look on his face and pointed to Fribble's notebook. "Are you sure you copied all that stuff down right?"

"Yes," Fribble said. "Why?"

"I think you made a mistake. I can't read big words, but I know all my numbers real well, and look." Scamper pointed accusingly at Fribble's notes. "You wrote down the same number for all those books. Even the grown-up books. How can that be? Doesn't each book have its own number so you can find it in the library?"

Miss Scurry said, "Good for you, Scamper. You're paying attention. Those are Dewey Decimal numbers. We use them to shelve all the books about a subject in one place in the library. So all of our books about knots have the number 623.8882 whether they are in the adult section or the children's book section. When you go to the shelf, all the 623.8882 books will be arranged alphabetically by the author's last name."

While Miss Scurry explained Dewey Decimals to Scamper, Fribble looked far across the room to the adult section of the library. It was a long way off, and it had lots and lots of books. He hoped he could find the right spot. Nervously, he tugged at his whiskers.

"Let me walk you over to the 600s in the adult section," Miss Scurry said.

Scamper took Miss Scurry's paw, and the three of them walked around tables and across the room.

"See those signs?" Miss Scurry pointed out signs at the end of each bookshelf. They had numbers on them. "Those numbers are like a map to help you find the way. Here it says '620.1 to 629.7.' Your books have numbers beginning with 623, so they'll be someplace in here."

Fribble dashed into the stacks until he found 623.8882. Then he started looking for the author's last name, Bertheir, and found *The Art of Knots: A Sailor's Handbook*.

"Here it is!" he shouted, forgetting to use his indoor voice. He clamped a paw over his mouth. Then he pulled the book off the shelf and handed it to Scamper. In a much quieter voice he asked, "Now, where is 'Derrick'?" He searched for that author's name until he saw *Great Knots and How to Tie Them*. Fribble pulled the book off the shelf, and they headed back to the children's area.

"I know how to look, now," Scamper said. Looking up at the signs at the ends of the book-shelves, he led them to the 600s where they soon found the children's book about knots.

A few minutes later, Fribble and Scamper were hurrying home with their three books. As soon as they reached the living room, Fribble put on the CD of sea shanties. He and Scamper put the board containing the knots on the floor between them, and began flipping through the pages of library books trying to find pictures of those very knots.

Almost immediately Fribble shouted, "Look! Here's one." He held a page of his illustrated book close to the board of knots.

"It's exactly like it," Scamper agreed. "What's its name?"

"It's called a bowline," Fribble said, "and it says you use it to make a loop to tie up a boat to a post at the pier."

"Write its name down," Scamper said.

Fribble got a pen, and he carefully printed "Bowline" on the little white tag glued beneath that knot.

Looking through the books, Fribble quickly found the anchor bend knot that ties a rope to an anchor, the reef knot that ties a sail cover onto the mainsail, the constrictor knot that pulls really tight, and the oysterman's stopper that ties off the end of a rope. Fribble carefully printed the names of the knots on the tags.

"Only two more to go," Fribble said, turning back to the book he was using.

Scamper yelled and jumped up and down when he discovered, all by himself, a sheepshank, a knot that is used to shorten a length of rope.

"Good for you," Fribble said. He wrote down the name on its white tag.

"What are you two doing?" Mother asked, coming in after hearing Scamper's squeaks of delight.

"We're finding all the knots on the knot board," Fribble explained.

"I thought you two would be investigating knots this evening," Mother said. "So I bought some rope when I was at the store today." She handed a piece of rope to each of them. "You can practice tying your knots."

"Hurrah!" Scamper said. "That's what we need! Thanks, Mom."

"Yeah, thanks! But before I can begin to practice tying the knots," Fribble said, taking the other rope and setting it beside him on the carpet, "there's one more knot that I have to find. It's this weird one." He picked up the heavy object that was covered with rope going around and around it. "So far, I haven't seen it in any of our books."

"I'm sure you'll find it," Mother said before she returned to the kitchen.

Scamper reluctantly put down his piece of rope and began looking for the strange knot in his library book. Fribble turned to the table of contents of his book and then opened to the section called "advanced knots." A few minutes later he stopped turning pages, and stared at a drawing while his heart beat fast.

"Here it is!" he said. "Look, Scamper! It's called a monkey's fist."

"A monkey's fist?" Scamper said. He stared suspiciously at the knot on the floor in front of him. "There's not a piece of a monkey inside that bunch of knots, is there?"

"'Course not," Fribble said. "It says here that you put a wooden ball or a rock in the middle. You tie this short rope to the end of a long line. The weight makes it easy for someone on a ship to throw it to someone on shore. Then the person on shore can haul in the longer rope and tie up the ship."

Fribble printed "Monkey's Fist" onto the tag of the knot.

Then he grabbed his piece of rope and said, "Now, let's tie knots!"

While Fribble and Scamper sat on the carpet practicing tying knots, the sea shanties CD played in the background.

"Have you picked out a favorite song yet? Are you going to teach one to your class?" Scamper asked.

"It's hard to choose," Fribble said. "Which one do you like best?"

"I like the one that goes, 'Oh, hi derry, hey derry, ho derry down.'" As Scamper sang loudly, he waved his paws in the air and rocked back and forth. "So merry, so merry, so merry are we."

"I like that one, too," Fribble said. "It's the chorus from a shanty called 'The Sailor's Alphabet.' But there are a lot of strange words in that shanty. It starts out easy enough with 'A is for anchor,' then there are lots of other words that I don't know, like B is for bowsprit, C is for capstan, and D is for davits, whatever they are."

"Couldn't you find out what those words mean?" Scamper asked.

"You're right. I should," Fribble admitted, "I guess I'm just being lazy. If I want my class to learn the song, I'll have to explain what the words mean." Fribble put down his rope. "In fact, I'll look them up right now. A good sailor doesn't put off his duty."

Fribble went and got the dictionary and brought it over to the table. Scamper climbed up on a chair beside him. It was a big dictionary, and there were lots of words on every page.

"Do you start in the beginning of the book and read all those words until you find the ones you want?" Scamper asked.

"No," Fribble said. "The words are in alphabetical order. The first word we want starts with 'b,' so we skip through all the As, and lots of the Bs. Then we start looking for b-o-w." As he spoke, Fribble flipped through pages of the dictionary, and then he ran his paw slowly down a page. Suddenly, his nose twitched.

"Here it is," Fribble said, "bowsprit." He read aloud to Scamper, "A large spar or pole sticking out from the bow or front of a boat."

Fribble wrote this down in his notebook.

Then he looked up "capstan." "Hey!!" Fribble said. "There's a little picture of it in the dictionary. It kind of looks like a fire plug that's narrow in the middle. It says you wind a rope or cable around the capstan to move or raise heavy weights." Fribble made more notes. "Now, what do you suppose a 'davit' is?"

Fribble paged through the dictionary until he found the word. "It's a crane for hoisting up ships in docks," he said, and he quickly made another note. "Now we know the ABCDs of sailing. That's enough for today!"

Fribble slammed shut the big dictionary, put it away, and happily went back to singing shanties and tying knots, using the leg of the coffee table to help him. Scamper sat next to him with his rope using another table leg to pull against.

A few minutes later, Scamper squeaked, "Help!"

Fribble stopped puzzling over the knot he was working on to look over at his brother. He quickly saw what had happened and did his best not to laugh. Somehow, Scamper had gotten tangled up in the rope and tied himself to the leg of the table. He was stuck. Fribble loosened the knots and untwisted the rope, freeing Scamper.

"I think it's time to tackle the monkey's fist!" Fribble said. "I'll bet we can tie that knot. Come on, Scamper. Help me find a good rock out in the backyard."

From the stone edging around one of the shrubs, Fribble found an almost round rock that fit nicely in his paw. They continued searching until they found another one that was the right size for Scamper. Then they came back inside and opened one of the books to the advanced knots section. This knot was tough. Fribble failed several times before he succeeded in following the directions. Even then, his knot was sort of lumpy and not as neat as the one in the book. Fribble helped Scamper tie his.

They raced out into the backyard again and tried throwing their monkey fists.

"Look how far it goes!" Scamper squeaked in joy as his monkey's fist sailed halfway across the yard.

When they got tired of throwing their monkey fists, they played catch with a baseball for a while before going back inside to practice tying the other knots again.

By the time Father came home to eat, Fribble could tie all of the sailor knots he'd found in the sea chest if he kept a library book open in front of him and followed the step-by-step instructions. With a little help, Scamper could, too. Before long, Fribble could tie all the knots without even looking at a book.

"Good work, Fribble!" Father said as he examined Fribble's latest knot. "Your Great Uncle Skipper Mouse will be really pleased when he sees how well you two can tie sailor knots when we go to visit him in June."

"June!" Fribble said, jumping up and swishing his tail wildly through the air. "That's next month. Are we really going that soon?"

Father smiled. "I phoned Great Uncle Skipper, and he said the sooner the better. No one at the office had signed up to take a vacation in early June, so I did. We're going to Maine on June 7, the day after school is out!"

"Yippeee!" Scamper shouted, and he did a little jig. "We're off to see the ocean!"

"I told Great Uncle Skipper about your careers project, Fribble, and he was so proud that you were learning about the life of a sailor." Father laughed. "He kept saying, 'I always knew that little Fribble was a sailor at heart!' And he said if you needed any help with your project, you could phone or write him."

Of course there was more sailor talk over dinner as Fribble told Mother and Father about the sailor's ABCDs from the sea shanty while Scamper talked about how far a monkey's fist would sail when you threw it.

"You'll have plenty of something specials to take to school," Mother said. "You can play the sea shanty and tie the sailor knots."

As soon as the table was cleared, Fribble said, "Now that I can tie all the knots, I get to open the next box in the sea chest. Anyone want to come watch?"

Everyone hurried into the living room where the old sea chest still rested on the floor in front of the couch.

Fribble turned the key in the lock, flung open the chest, and took out box number two. He used a scissors to cut the sturdy twine wrapped around the box. Then he lifted the lid and pulled back the tissue paper. Sitting on top of a heap of colorful cloth was a beautiful little wooden box. The dark wood box was carved with designs of spouting whales, fish, and mermaids.

"Oooh!" Scamper said. His eyes were shining. "Open it, Fribble! Open it!"

Fribble's nose twitched, his paw trembled a bit, and he found himself holding his breath as he carefully opened the small, wooden box.

"Wow!" Fribble exhaled as he peeked. "Wow!"

Resting inside the red-velvet-lined box was something about the size of a fat pencil. Curled around it was a long chain. Both were made of shiny brass. Fribble reached in and took out the object and looked at it carefully.

"What is it?" Scamper asked, edging in closer.

"I don't know yet," Fribble said. "It kind of looks like a whistle." He raised it to his mouth and blew hard in one end. It made a high-pitched shrill blast. Mother flung her paws over her ears.

"It is a whistle." Scamper smiled broadly. "A real loud one."

Fribble put the shiny whistle down and looked to see what else was in the bottom of box number two. One by one he lifted out four square pieces of folded cloth about as big as giant napkins. One was white and blue with a notch cut out of one end. One was all red and it had a notch cut out of it, too. One had a blue-striped top and bottom with a white stripe in the middle. And the last square was divided into two triangles. One triangle was red and the other was yellow.

"These look like flags," Fribble said, "but mysterious flags. I'll bet sailors use these on ships for something."

Then Fribble noticed that once again Great Uncle Skipper Mouse had taped a card inside the lid of the box. Fribble tore it off. Instead of being printed, this note was in Great Uncle Skipper's spidery handwriting. It was hard to read, so Fribble handed it to his mother. She put on her reading glasses.

"'Dear Fribble,'" she read aloud, "'Sailors use signals on their ship, and they also signal from one ship to another, and from ship to shore. Can you figure out how this whistle works and how these signal flags are used? Great Uncle Skipper.'"

"'Course I can," Fribble said. "I'll look them up on the Internet. Can I use our computer?" he asked.

Father glanced at the clock. "It's bedtime in an hour, but you can use it and learn what you can until then."

Fribble stuffed the flags and whistle back in the box and raced to the family computer in the study. Scamper ran along with him. Fribble typed "sailor's whistle," into the computer's search engine and waited to see what came up. The first item was "boatswain's whistle, usually called a bosun's whistle."

Fribble read out loud to Scamper, "'A bosun's whistle has been used by sailors for over 500 years. The bosun blows different signals to let the sailors know when it's all hands on deck or time for lights out.' Oh, boy! I'm going to learn how to blow signals on this from my room to your room. I'll be able to signal you, Scamper. I'll blow the whistle when it's time to stop reading and turn lights out."

"Can I blow it, too, sometimes?" Scamper asked.

"When I know how, I'll teach you," Fribble promised. "Now for the flags."

It didn't take Fribble long to get to a colorful page on the computer screen that showed International Signal Flags that are used by sailors all over the world.

"They're every color of the rainbow," Scamper squeaked.

But Fribble was reading the article above the flags on the page. "No. Not every color," he said. "It says here that signal flags are red, white, blue, yellow, or black."

"Hey! Isn't that one exactly like one that's in your sea chest?" Scamper pointed to a picture of a flag on the screen.

"It sure is," Fribble agreed. "It says this flag that's half blue and half white means there is a diver beneath the ship. Keep clear."

Fribble drew a picture of the flag onto his notebook page along with its meaning.

"The red and yellow triangle flag means 'man overboard,'" Fribble explained. "And look! That solid red one means 'explosives.'" Fribble made more notes.

Fribble scanned the rest of the flags until he found the last one he was looking for. It had a blue-striped top and bottom with a white stripe in the middle. "This one means 'ship on fire,'" he said.

Mother walked into the room just then. "How is your research coming along?" Fribble told her what each of the flags meant. "And this," he added, opening the small wooden box, "is a bosun's whistle. I'm going to learn how to blow it."

"I'm sure you are," Mother agreed. "But not tonight. It's time for bed. You may read for five minutes, and then it's lights out."

Fribble whispered something in Scamper's ear before they each left for their rooms. Five minutes later, after they were both in bed, and Mother had gone back downstairs, there was one blast of the bosun's whistle from Fribble's room. This was followed by giggles, and suddenly it was lights out upstairs.

"Could I borrow a piece of writing paper?"
Fribble asked Mother as he ate his snack after
school the next day. "I want to write a letter to Great
Uncle Skipper."

"What a good idea," Mother said. "He'll be happy
to hear from you."

She fetched the paper while Fribble cleared the
table and got his pen and some magic markers. He
wrote, "Thank you for the sea chest, Great Uncle
Skipper. I have opened two boxes so far. I can tie
all the knots. Scamper can, too. The monkey's fist
was hardest. I like the signal flags and know what
they mean." Fribble drew little pictures of the signal
flags with notes underneath each one. He colored
the flags with his magic markers. "I can't play the

bosun's whistle yet, but I'm going to learn. I blow it every night to tell Scamper when it's time for lights out! We can hardly wait to see you next month. Love, Fribble."

As Fribble wrote, Scamper drew a picture of an ocean that he wanted Fribble to include with the letter. Fribble got Uncle Skipper's address from his mother, printed it on an envelope, and added a stamp. Then Fribble did his school homework without having to be reminded. He wanted to have his whole evening free to learn more about what else was in the sea chest.

At dinner Fribble said, "We're making career puppets at school."

"What's a career puppet?" Father asked.

"Mine's a puppet of a sailor," Fribble said. "We taped a short tube inside a ball of rolled-up newspaper to make puppet heads. Then we put the tubes over necks of pop bottles to hold the puppet heads up, while we added more newspaper to make noses and ears. After that, we dipped strips of papers in wallpaper paste and pasted these all around the head until it was smooth. Once it's dry, we'll paint the face and dress the puppet. Tweek's going to dress his as a pianist in a tuxedo. On Career Night, our puppets will sit on our tables along with our something specials."

"Do you get to keep the puppet and play with it?" Scamper wanted to know.

"Sure," Fribble said. "I'm going to take mine to show Great Uncle Skipper." His whiskers quivered in excitement as he turned to his mother. "I brought a pattern home for the puppet suit, Mother. Will you help me find some sailor cloth for it? Mrs. Tremble says parents can help."

"Yes," Mother said. "I'll be glad to help. I have some blue material around here somewhere, I think. I'll look for it." Fribble's mother did a lot of sewing. His favorite Great Aunt Squeegee had taught her.

As soon as dinner was over, Fribble announced, "Time to open another box from the sea chest."

Father, Mother, and Scamper joined Fribble in the living room where he threw open the big trunk and took out box number three. He opened the lid and saw that this box was extra full of tissue paper. Carefully, he began unwrapping and found two objects, each wrapped in more tissue.

"Whatever this is," Fribble said, picking one of the objects up, "it's very light." Finally, when the last piece of tissue was removed, Fribble held in his paws a small, clear glass bottle with a cork in it. Inside the bottle was a tiny ship. He gasped but held his paws very still as his tail whipped through the air in excitement.

"Oh, my gosh! How did someone ever make this?"

There were three masts with white sails with black stripes billowing out, and there were more sails in the front and in the back of the boat. Flying from the center mast was an itty-bitty flag.

Fribble oohed and aahed while holding the bottle carefully in his paws and looking at it from all sides before gently handing it to Scamper, who was squirming about in his eagerness to get hold of it.

"Hey! This ship is lots bigger than the hole in the bottle," Scamper said. "How did it get inside?" Without waiting for an answer, he asked, "Do you think Great Uncle Skipper built it? Is it one of the ships he sailed on? What kind of a ship is it, do you think?"

"Whoa!" Fribble said. "Slow down, Scamper. I don't know. Not yet. But I'm going to find out." Fribble took the ship in a bottle back from Scamper and handed it to his mother and father on the couch so they could admire it, too.

"Let's see what else is in this box." He reached inside and pulled out the other tissue-wrapped object. Carefully Fribble unwrapped a smooth, golden-white object attached to a driftwood stand. The white rock, or whatever it was, stood up tall like a statue. Carved into it was a black-line drawing of a ship. And in front of the ship was the tail of a whale, disappearing into the waves.

"Will you look at this!" Fribble said. He turned the object over in his paws. "I don't know if it's a rock, or maybe a bone."

"I don't know, either." Mother reached over and ran her paw up and down the smooth side. "I wonder what it is?"

Fribble looked in the lid of the shoebox. Sure enough, there was a printed note from Great Uncle Skipper. Fribble read it out loud. "'Dear Fribble, I built this ship in a bottle. Can you figure out how? She's called the *Lucy Ann*. And what do you suppose this white carving is made of? I'll give you a clue. It was carved long ago by a sailor who took it from a big animal that swims in the sea. Love, Great Uncle Skipper.'"

"Two more mysteries, Fribble," Scamper said. "And two more something specials you can take to school to show everybody on career night."

"First I have to find out more about them," Fribble said. "Is it all right if I use the computer?"

"Of course," his mother said. She looked at the wall clock. "You have a little while until bedtime. Before you go, though, please give me your puppet-suit pattern, and I'll look to see if I have some cloth for your sailor suit."

Fribble got the puppet pattern from the notebook in his backpack and gave it to his mother. He hurried off to the study where he called up the search engine. Then he just sat there, staring at the computer screen.

Scamper sat beside him, and after a minute when Fribble still did nothing, he impatiently asked, "Why don't you start hunting for it, Fribble?"

"Hunting for what?" Fribble asked.

"That white thing, with the ship carved on it."

"That's my problem," Fribble said. "I don't know what the 'white thing' is. How can I type it in and search for it, if I don't know what to call it?"

"Type in 'white thing,'" Scamper said.

Fribble shook his head. "That's not enough. A pillow on the bed might be a 'white thing.' We have to describe it better than that."

"How about 'white rock sea'?" Scamper said.

"I don't think so," Fribble said. "But I'll try." He entered "white rock sea" into the search engine. Up came listings for White Rock Beach, White Rock Resort, White Rock clothing.

"No, that's not helping us," Fribble said. He furrowed his brow. "It looks like a bone to me. Great Uncle Skipper said some sailor long ago carved it from an animal that lived in the sea." As he continued to think, Fribble stroked his long whiskers.

"Let's see," he finally said. Slowly he typed "sailor's bone carving." He held his breath and waited.

Almost immediately a whole list of Web sites came up. The very first one showed a picture of an object a lot like the one from the sea chest. Fribble quickly read aloud to Scamper. "'Anything that's carved by sailors on ivory, bone, or sea shells is called "scrimshaw." When sailors went to sea for a long time, they carved these to have something to do.'" He skipped ahead, reading rapidly. "Hey! The one that looks just like ours is a tooth from a whale! Can you believe it?" Fribble jumped out of the chair. "We've got a tooth from a whale that was caught by sailors long, long ago."

Fribble went running, his tail held high behind him and Scamper in hot pursuit, out to the living room where Father was reading the newspaper and Mother was looking in her sewing basket. Both listened as Fribble poured out his news about scrimshaw.

"Now," Fribble said, preparing to run back to the computer, "I'm going to try to find out about building ships in bottles."

Mother glanced at the wall clock again. "It's bedtime. Ships in bottles will have to wait until tomorrow. Off you go now. Lights out in ten minutes."

Before Fribble went up the stairs to his room, he picked up the whale tooth and carried it with him. He set it right on his bedside table beside his clock. He re-read parts of his library book, *John Paul Jones, America's Sailor*. Before he turned out the light, he blew loudly on his bosun's whistle to signal lights out to Scamper.

⤙⊷⊷○⊶⊶⤚

The next day after school, Fribble picked up his little brother and took him to the art room to see his career puppet head. Fribble found it, with his name taped to the bottle, on the shelf, all dry and smooth.

"Doesn't look much like a sailor to me," Scamper said.

On hearing Scamper, Miss Sketch, the art teacher, smiled. "It isn't finished yet, but it's a good beginning. Fribble can already see a handsome sailor when he looks at that puppet head."

"Wait until you see it dressed up in a sailor suit," Fribble said.

Then Fribble told Miss Sketch all about the little ship in the bottle.

"I'm going on the computer tonight to learn how people can build boats in little bottles. I want to learn more about the big ships that people sailed in, too. Those old wooden ships look pretty complicated to me," Fribble said. "I can't picture what it was like inside a real ship. Where did everyone sleep and eat?"

"Maybe to learn about the inside of an old-time whaling ship, you need a special book with diagrams," Miss Sketch suggested.

"What's a diagram?" Fribble asked.

"A diagram is a detailed line drawing or picture. The diagram of a ship would show you exactly what it looked like inside. I'll bet Miss Longwhiskers, the librarian, will help you find a book that has diagrams in it if you ask her."

"Thanks, Miss Sketch." Fribble and Scamper ran off to the library to find Miss Longwhiskers and tell her what they were looking for.

She went to the card catalog and asked Fribble to type in "wooden ships." Up came a title with the Dewey Decimal number of 623.82. Fribble hurried to the nonfiction section and found the book on the shelf.

"Wow! This is going to be great." Fribble quickly rifled through the pages. "Look! It's got lots of pictures, I mean, diagrams, of the inside of the ship." He checked out the book, and he and Scamper hurried home.

Mother had a snack waiting for them, a bowl of salty crackers and pieces of Muenster cheese, Fribble's favorite. As soon as he finished, Scamper ran next door to play with a friend. Fribble lingered over yet another piece of cheese.

"Great Uncle Skipper called today," Mother said. "I told him how you are learning so much from his sea chest, Fribble. He said since you are so good at figuring things out that he's mailing you something else to work on."

"Did he say what it was?" Fribble asked.

"He did mention something about a treasure map," she said, smiling.

"A treasure map! A real treasure map?" Fribble shouted.

"We'll have to wait and see, won't we?" Mother said.

"I hope he sent it overnight," Fribble said.

Fribble brushed crumbs off his whiskers and went to the computer to look up "model ships in bottles." There were many pages showing how the parts of a ship were built outside the bottle. The masts and sails were tiny pieces, laid on top of the hull, with threads attached to them. Once the ship was put inside the bottle, you had to pull the right threads very carefully to get the masts and the sails up and in place. Fribble marveled at how much work, patience, and skill it took.

Satisfied that he knew how ships got into bottles, Fribble went to his room with his new library book and looked at the diagrams showing the inside of an old-time wooden whaling ship. But thoughts of Great Uncle Skipper's treasure map made it hard for him to concentrate. Fribble lay back on his bed and closed his eyes. He dreamed of sailing on the ocean waves and seeing a whale just ahead of him in the ocean. Then he imagined going ashore with a treasure map in hand. What would he find?

Fribble wasted no time the next afternoon in collecting Scamper after school and heading home. There was no dropping by the art room looking at puppet heads or stopping in the library for books today. In fact, Fribble was walking so fast that Scamper had to run along beside his brother to keep up.

Panting a little, Scamper finally asked, "Hey! What's the hurry?"

"If Great Uncle Skipper sent the treasure map by overnight mail, it may already be waiting at our house," Fribble explained, keeping up his rapid pace.

On hearing that, Scamper stopped questioning and simply jogged along, keeping up with Fribble's quick steps.

As soon as he opened the door of their house, Fribble rushed up to his mother in the kitchen and asked, "Did anything come for me in the mail?"

Mother smiled and pointed to the kitchen table. An after-school snack was waiting there. So was a big envelope addressed to Fribble from Great Uncle Skipper Mouse. Fribble's eyes shone and his tail lashed through the air as he raced to the table, whipped off his book bag, dropped it on an empty chair, and tore open the big brown envelope.

Out tumbled two things: a letter and another smaller envelope. Fribble began reading the letter aloud to Scamper and Mother.

"'Dear Fribble, You and Scamper are super sleuths! Are you sure you're not planning to grow up to be detectives? You're doing a great job of figuring out about all the mysterious things in the sea chest. Good for you! Thank you for the picture you sent of the ship signal flags and what they mean, and please tell Scamper how much I liked his drawing of the ship at sea.'"

Scamper, who had been listening carefully to every word of Great Uncle Skipper's letter, puffed out his little chest and nodded his head when he heard this.

"I knew he'd love my picture," he said.

Fribble continued reading. "'I can't wait to see you all. In fact, I'm marking off the days on my calendar.'"

Fribble looked at his mother and smiled as they both glanced over at the big calendar hanging in their kitchen where Fribble had also been marking off the days until June 7. Each morning before his first bite of breakfast, he crossed out a day.

Fribble went on. "'I'm proud that on Career Night you'll be telling people about the life of a sailor! I'm sending you a copy of a treasure map in the enclosed sealed envelope, but don't open it until you've finished with everything in the sea chest and Career Night is all over. Then, if you have time, you can take a peek at the map. If you don't have time to open it before June 7, be sure to bring it with you. I'll help you with the treasure hunt! Lots of love, Great Uncle Skipper Mouse.'"

Fribble picked up the smaller sealed envelope. It was marked "Treasure Map." Fribble's nose twitched and his whiskers quivered. With his bright eyes he searched the envelope hoping to find a little crack or tear that might let him peek inside.

"You don't get to open it yet, Fribble," Scamper reminded him, as Fribble kept turning the envelope over and over in his paws.

"I know," Fribble said. He sat down in front of his snack and propped the sealed envelope up against his glass of milk. Nibbling away, he stared at the envelope as if he had X-ray vision and could read what it said inside.

As soon as he finished his snack, Scamper ran off to play with his friend, Twitter.

Fribble called, "Don't you have any homework to do tonight?"

"Nope," Scamper said, and ran out the door.

Fribble sighed. "First graders have it so easy."

"Yes," his mother agreed, "but they don't get to make career puppets." She walked over to her sewing basket and pulled out a finished sailor suit. It was navy blue with a white collar and stripes. "Do you like it?"

Fribble grinned as he picked up the little suit in his paws. He held it up and looked at it from every direction.

"It's perfect! Thanks, Mom. We're going to put yarn hair and paint faces on our puppets tomorrow. As soon as that's done, we can put on their suits! Wow! Mine will be great!"

"If you'll measure around the puppet's head and tell me how many inches it is, I'll make a little sailor hat, too!" Mother said.

"Thanks, Mom!" Fribble handed back his puppet suit, picked up his backpack, and headed up to his room. "I've got a ton of math to do tonight."

"Ah, but you're so quick at math, Fribble," Mother pointed out. "You'll have it done in no time at all."

Fribble wanted to pull another package out of the sea chest, not sit at his desk and do math. But he knew the whole family enjoyed the packages and that he really should wait until his father got home. So he sat at his desk in his room, pulled out a math book, and went straight to work. His mother was right. His assignment was all finished by the time she called him for dinner even though after each problem, he stopped to look over at the envelope on his bedside table.

That night, as soon as the family finished eating and he had helped clear away the dishes from their yummy macaroni and cheese feast, Fribble led the way to the living room and removed the last box from the old sea chest.

This box was a little bigger and a little heavier than the other three boxes had been. Fribble lifted it out and sat with it on the floor in front of the couch. Scamper snuggled so close, he was almost in Fribble's lap.

Mother and Father leaned forward and Fribble's whiskers trembled as he untied the knot, lifted off the cover, and pulled out something square wrapped in tissue. He pulled away the paper to reveal a wooden box. Inside the box was a shiny, heavy piece of brass.

"Is it a clock?" Scamper asked, sitting up on his knees and leaning over Fribble to get a good look at the object.

"No," Fribble said. "It has a hand like a clock, but it doesn't have a clock face." He turned it around. "See, it has lots and lots of lines on it in black, blue, green, and red. And look! This hand keeps pointing in one direction." He leaned in closer. "It's pointing north! I think I know what this is! It's a compass, isn't it, Dad?"

Fribble held it up to his father, who examined it carefully before handing it to Fribble's mother. "Yes, you're right. It's a mariner's compass," he said.

Fribble lifted out a second wrapped package. This time it was another brass instrument of some kind in a wooden stand.

"Is this one a clock?" Scamper wanted to know.

"It's got a hand on it," Fribble said, "but it only has four numbers: 28, 29, 30, and 31." He scratched his head with a paw in puzzlement.

Scamper asked, "Whoever heard of 29 o'clock?"

"I don't think it is a clock," Fribble said. "See? It's got words on it." With his paw he pointed out the words to his little brother. "Stormy, Rain, Change, Fair, Very Dry. It sounds as if it has something to do with the weather."

"A thurmurer?" asked Scamper. "To tell how hot or cold it is."

"You mean a thermometer," Fribble corrected him. "No, if it were a thermometer, it would have lots more numbers on it."

"Well, what is it then?" Scamper demanded.

"I don't know yet," Fribble said. "But it's something a good sailor must need to tell him about the weather. I'll find out."

Father and Mother looked at the newest object, too, but they didn't say anything.

"There's one more thing in the package," Scamper said.

Fribble lifted the last object out of the box. "It's real heavy, too," he said. Quickly he tore away the paper. In his paws he held another wooden box. It was a deep-red mahogany with a brass anchor decorating the lid.

"Maybe this is a clock," Scamper whispered hopefully, as Fribble opened the box.

But when Fribble looked inside, he could tell right away it wasn't a clock. Carefully, he picked up a heavy tube covered in black leather and held it in his paw. At each end of the tube, there was a piece of clear glass. Scamper crowded over to stare into the piece of glass. "Is it a mirror? I can see my eye, I think."

Fribble looked at the smaller end of the tube and tugged. To his surprise, that end pulled out, farther and farther, making one long tube of four brass sections. The leather section at the end, holding a big piece of glass, was the biggest. Fribble pointed the long brass tube at his mother and peered into the little end.

"Oooh," he gasped. "Mom! Your eyes are so big!" He put the long tube in his lap and stared at it. "I've seen these in pirate movies. It's a spyglass!"

For a few minutes, everyone handed the spyglass around.

Fribble looked at the clock. "Is it all right if I use the computer and try to find out what this thing is?" He pointed to the brass object that had 28, 29, 30, and 31 on it.

"Couldn't it wait until tomorrow?" Mother asked.

"If I know what it is, I can read about it during my library period at school tomorrow," Fribble said.

In the study in front of the computer, Fribble wondered what to enter into the search engine. He was sure this object had something to do with weather. Finally he entered "weather 28, 29, 30, 31." Whiskers quivering, Fribble sat in front of the computer screen waiting to see what would pop up.

Suddenly the screen showed "Singapore Weather Forecast, High, 30 Degrees C." A bunch of highs and lows of 28, 29, 30, and 31 showed up for other cities, too.

Scamper looked first at the screen and then at his brother's downcast face. "That's not what we want, is it?"

"No," Fribble said. "I'll have to enter something else. I think it has something to do with weather. I'll

try 'weather measuring instruments.'" He typed this in and waited.

A site called weather instruments came up with information and pictures.

"Look," Scamper squeaked. "There's a thurmurer!"

"Right," Fribble said. "And look what's right below the thermometer." He pointed to an object exactly like the one from the sea chest. "It's called a barometer."

"Hurrah!" Scamper shouted. "Now you'll know what to hunt for in the library."

>·+‹›·O·‹›·+·‹

The next day, during library period, Fribble returned his book, and then asked Miss Longwhiskers, the librarian, "Where's the best place to learn something about a compass, a barometer, and a spyglass?"

"You always have the most interesting questions, Fribble," Miss Longwhiskers said. "You might want to start in the set of encyclopedias. That will tell you quite a bit, and then you could enter those words into our computer catalog and see if we have any books that could tell you more, like how to use a compass."

Fribble headed for the set of encyclopedias. One by one, he looked up the various instruments, scribbling notes as fast as he could into his spiral notebook. Then, looking at the library clock and finding he had only five minutes left, he hurried to the computer catalog and typed in "how to use a compass."

Nothing came up. Fribble wasn't discouraged. He knew sometimes it took a while to find just the right words to get to the book he wanted. He asked himself, What do you use a compass for? And he answered, To find your way.

This time he entered "compass find way." To his delight, two books came up. One was called *Finding Your Way* and the other was called *Tools of Navigation: 15 Activities*. Fribble jotted down their call numbers and checked them out.

After school, Fribble had no homework for a change, so he quickly settled down to read his two books. By dinnertime, he was bursting with information. "I'm learning all about orienteering," he informed everyone.

"What's that?" Scamper wanted to know.

"It's learning how to use a compass and a map," Fribble explained.

"What did you learn about the compass, barometer, and spyglass?" Mother asked.

"The compass is an old Chinese invention," Fribble explained. "An Italian scientist built the first barometer. It measures air pressure. And a Dutch eyeglass maker made the first spyglass so sailors could look for enemy ships."

"Wow!" Dad said. "People all over the world have been interested in sailing, haven't they?"

"Yeah," Fribble said.

That night Fribble counted off the days until Career Night, next Wednesday. And on Saturday, they'd be in Maine. Fribble was determined to get a peek at the map before they left. Would he be able to find his way to the treasure?

Though Fribble was tempted, he followed Great Uncle Skipper's instructions and kept the treasure map sealed in its envelope. He pinned it up on the bulletin board in his bedroom. Every night, even though he couldn't see it in the dark, Fribble looked over to where he knew the envelope containing the map was hanging, and his little heart beat faster. Soon, he thought, soon I'll be searching for treasure!

On Friday, Fribble showed his mother the finished puppet head that he'd brought home from school. "I have to bring it back to school on Wednesday, all dressed, and with my special somethings. That day we'll get everything ready in class to share with all our friends and relatives who are coming to school for Career Night."

"You did a great job in painting your puppet face, Fribble." Mother beamed. "I think this little sailor mouse looks just like you!"

Fribble stroked his long whiskers with satisfaction. He wondered if he and his sea-faring puppet looked anything like Great Uncle Skipper Mouse. He hoped so.

Fribble glued the collar of the sailor suit onto the cardboard neck that hung out of the papier mâché puppet head. He set his puppet on the kitchen table where it smiled up at him. Fribble circled around, looking at his puppet approvingly from all angles.

"Now, all he needs is a sailor hat," Fribble announced.

Fribble helped Mother use the sewing tape to measure the circumference of the puppet's head. Mother jotted down the measurement.

"What kind of a hat do you want?"

"Gosh, I don't know," Fribble said.

"Why don't you find a picture of one you like?" Mother suggested. "Some sailors wear small white hats. Admirals of long ago wore big black hats. I'll need to know what you want before I try to make a hat for your puppet."

Fribble rushed off to the computer to do a search for naval hats. Scamper soon joined him there.

"Whatcha looking for?" Scamper wanted to know.

"I'm picking out a hat for my sailor puppet," Fribble explained.

Up on the computer screen were pictures of all kinds of sailor hats dating from the present day to way back in history. One was the popular white Dixie-cup style that so many sailors wear, and another was a fancy tricorn with feathers. There was a captain's hat with a braid and a gold anchor on the visor, and there were fancy black felt pirates' hats decorated with skulls and crossbones.

"Some of these hats are really awesome," Scamper said. His nose twitched. "Which one are you going to pick?"

"I don't know." Fribble's tail flipped back and forth. "It's hard to choose." Unable to decide, he finally printed out the page of pictures and scurried out to the kitchen to show his mother.

"Ah," Mother said, carefully wiping cheese puff pastry from her paws before taking the piece of paper. "So many hats! Which one do you want?"

Fribble hesitated. "Since it's Career Night, I guess it would be better to choose to be a captain or an admiral than a pirate, wouldn't it?"

Mother smiled. "You have a point."

"I like that one best." Scamper said, pointing to a pirate's hat with a red feather and a white skull and crossbones.

"I like it, too," Fribble said. "But this is the one I want for Career Night." He pointed out the captain's hat, with visor and gold braid. "Can you make it?"

His mother smiled. "Your Great Aunt Squeegee taught me. She's a fantastic hat maker. I promise I'll have a hat ready for you to take back to school on Monday."

Now that he knew his puppet would be dressed and looking great for Wednesday, Fribble turned his attention to his special somethings.

He got out the ropes his mother had bought. He and Scamper sat on the floor and practiced tying knots. Scamper was kind of silly, giggling and tying up his stuffed animals to chair legs. But Fribble was serious, trying to remember all he'd learned. His whiskers quivered as he concentrated on the monkey's fist.

After dinner, he and Scamper tooted on the bosun's whistle until his mother suggested that maybe they'd like to go outside to practice for a while.

All weekend, Fribble was either busy with homework or practicing for Career Night. Mother was busy, too, sewing and beginning to plan everything that needed to be done before they left on their trip next Friday.

Monday night after the dishes were cleared away from the table, Father said, "Here's a map. Anyone want to help me plan our route from Cheddarville to Maine?"

Mother, Fribble, and Scamper all crowded around the table.

Fribble leaned up onto the table to get a good look at the map. He smiled as he put his paw on Cheddarville, and then he looked for Maine.

"The little box here in the corner of the map gives lots of information," Father explained, as he pointed to the map legend. "See, it says that an inch equals 30 miles. How many miles do you think it is between here and Great Uncle Skipper?"

Fribble looked at all the roads and traced along what he thought looked like the shortest one from one place to the other.

"The road is crooked," he complained. "I can't really tell how many inches it is."

"You could use a piece of string," Father suggested. "Lay it along the route, and then measure it."

Fribble hopped up to get a piece of string. He measured one route and then another, before everyone agreed on the shortest way to travel.

When it was time to go to bed, Fribble was so excited about the trip he found it hard to fall asleep.

On Tuesday night, with help from Scamper, Fribble packed a small suitcase for school. He put in an extension cord and a little tape player mother loaned him along with the tape his music teacher made of his class singing the "The Sailor's Alphabet."

"I'll play that sea shanty as background music at my table," Fribble explained.

Fribble smoothed the signal flags at the bottom of the suitcase and put the board of knots on top of them. Then, using tissue paper, he packed up the spyglass, the mariner's compass, the barometer, the scrimshaw whale tooth, the ship in a bottle, and the bosun's whistle.

"Are you going to take the treasure map?" Scamper asked.

"No," Fribble said. His whiskers quivered, and his eyes darted around the room as he whispered, "Treasure maps are secret."

Scamper nodded.

"That's it," Fribble finally said, snapping the suit-case shut.

Fribble tossed and turned that night, but he finally fell asleep. First thing in the morning he hurried down to breakfast, carrying his suitcase with him. He rushed over to look at his sailor puppet, which sat on the kitchen counter wearing a hand-some white captain's hat with black visor and a gold braid trim.

"Wow!" he said. "Thanks, Mom. It looks great!"

Fribble nibbled at a piece of toast, but he was too excited to eat much.

"I'll drive you to school this morning," Mother said. "You have a lot to carry."

Scamper got his backpack, while Fribble picked up his suitcase in one hand and slipped his other paw into his puppet.

"Ready?" Mother asked.

"Aye, aye!" Fribble said, moving the puppet head as he spoke.

At school, it was hard to concentrate on lessons in the morning. In the afternoon, Mrs. Tremble didn't even try to teach. She had the children help her get the room ready for their families and friends to come and visit. They moved chairs and tables into place, and all the students were assigned a spot to put their puppets and something specials. Tweek was set up right next to Fribble.

"Hey! I like your concert pianist," Fribble said, looking at Tweek's puppet dressed in a tuxedo with a black bow tie. Tweek also had pictures of famous pianists and sheet music to display along with his written report.

"I like your sailor, too," Tweek said. He looked over Fribble's treasures from the sea chest. Several other students crowded around and Fribble was eager to show off his things.

Mrs. Tremble said, "Doors open promptly at 7:00. Each of you should get here a little early and be ready to share your reports and your something specials."

That evening, Fribble dressed in his best clothes to go to school. While his parents went to the school art show, Fribble hurried to his classroom and stood behind his table. Everything was set.

Fribble paced nervously back and forth behind his table. He checked the tape recorder and counted his eight something specials from the sea chest one more time. The barometer, mariner's compass, ship in a bottle, scrimshaw, signal flags, spyglass, and knots. Suddenly he froze. He counted again. There were only seven! What was missing? The bosun's whistle was gone! The red case that once held it was gaping open, empty.

Fribble's tail lashed back and forth as he began a hasty search. It hadn't fallen on the floor. It wasn't on Tweek's table or on the table on the other side of him.

Fribble tried hard not to panic but his nose twitched. He rushed to Mrs. Tremble.

"My bosun's whistle is gone!" he said.

"It can't be far," Mrs. Tremble said. "Let me help you look for it."

Mrs. Tremble came over to the table, and the two of them looked together. Tweek joined in the search, too.

Suddenly from somewhere came a loud whistle. Fribble would recognize that sound anywhere. It was his bosun's whistle! Looking across the room, Fribble spied Scamper with Twitter. They were standing in front of Twitter's sister's table, and Scamper was blowing the whistle loudly to show how it worked.

Fribble raced across the room. As he ran, he thought of how he was going to scold his little brother.

But just as he got there, Scamper turned, glowing with pride, as he announced, "And here he is now, my big brother, Captain Fribble Mouse. I was just showing off your bosun's whistle, Captain, and telling them that you're teaching me to blow signals on it, too, even though I'm not as good as you are yet."

Fribble's anger left as quickly as it had come. Instead of calling his brother names, Fribble said, "C'mon, Scamper. We've got to go get ready."

Parents and friends soon came and worked their way around the room. There was always a crowd at Fribble's table, watching and nodding, as he tied knots; waved signal flags; and showed off the ship-in-the-bottle, spyglass, barometer, compass, and whale tooth. Every now and then, Fribble even let Scamper toot the bosun's whistle for him.

By 8:30, Fribble and his family were back home again.

"Great job, Fribble!" Father said as he helped Fribble store his puppet and his treasures in the sea chest, which was now in Fribble's bedroom.

They all gathered back in the kitchen for a late-night snack of coconut cream cheese balls that mother had made.

In mid-bite, Fribble suddenly jumped up and said, "Career Night is over! It's time to open the treasure map!" He ran to his bedroom to pull it off the bulletin board.

Fribble charged down the stairs and almost flew into the kitchen, clutching the precious treasure map, still in its envelope, in his paws. He leaped onto his seat at the table and, as Father, Mother, and Scamper watched, he tore open the envelope. Inside, neatly folded, was a large sheet of paper.

Fribble carefully unfolded the map and smoothed it out into the center of the table. It was hand drawn in black ink. At the top, it said "Treasure Map." On the right-hand side were lots of wavy lines marked "Atlantic Ocean." There was a faint line going from top to bottom and another line that went across the map, and Fribble wondered what the big numbers on these lines could mean. Several street and road names were on the upper left-hand side of the page. A dotted line led from a little house drawn on Bay Street to a big "X" in the middle of the map.

Scamper squeaked aloud and almost toppled off his chair when he first saw the X. He plopped his paw on it. "That must be where the treasure is! 'X' marks the spot!"

Fribble's tail lashed through the air as he tried to take in everything about the map at once.

"Look! It's got a map legend," he said, pointing to the top corner. There was a scale of miles that read: one inch equals two miles.

"And what does that say?" Scamper pointed to words at the bottom of the page.

Fribble cleared his throat and read it out loud:

"You start at a cottage, all grey like a gull,
And make your way close by the sea,
Race over the white sand, and remember that
The map in your paws holds the key.

There on the spot, standing high on a cliff,
One eye winking very brightly.
Climb up and up until you reach
Eleven and twenty-three.

Now look in the crack that's just to your left,
A shiny small treasure you'll see!
You'll hold in your paw a fine souvenir,
A piece of our great history."

Fribble scratched his head, stroked his whiskers, and read it again to himself. "What's it mean?" Scamper scratched his head, too.

"These are clues," Fribble said, his nose twitching. "It will take some time to study them."

"Yes, it will," Mother agreed, "but not tonight. You've had a big day, and tomorrow is another big day. I'll finish packing clothes for all of us while you two are at school in the morning picking up your report cards and saying good-bye to your friends and teachers. When you get home, you may each add one small suitcase of toys or books, or whatever you want to bring along. We'll have lunch and then as fast as we can manage, we'll leave for Maine to see Great Uncle Skipper!"

"With a late start, we won't get far the first day," Father said, "but we'll be off. That's the important thing. The hardest part of any trip is locking the front door and leaving the house!"

"So, to bed right now you two," Mother said. "Your treasure map clues will have to wait a little while longer."

Minutes later, Fribble blew the bosun's whistle, and it was lights out.

School was a beehive of activity the next morning. Mrs. Tremble handed out a big shopping bag to each student. Fribble filled his with all the things he still had in his desk—stubby pencils, broken crayons, a used-up bottle of glue, scissors, and a ruler—all things that he wanted to take home with him. He threw away crumpled papers and handed in school books.

Fribble gave Mrs. Tremble a hug along with a little package his mother had sent, and he said good-bye to Tweek, promising he'd send him a post-card from Maine.

"Will you bring a seashell back for me?" Tweek asked.

"I will," Fribble promised.

Fribble hurried to the first grade room where Scamper was saying good-bye to Twitter. For blocks around the school, the air was filled with happy chatter as everyone hurried home to begin summer vacation.

As soon as Fribble and Scamper entered the kitchen at home, Mother said, "Let's finish packing before we have lunch. I've put a little suitcase on each of your beds. You can pack whatever you want to play with, but remember, only what will fit in the one bag. All right? And Fribble, you help your brother."

Fribble had been thinking about what to take with him for several days, so it didn't take him long. He packed the sea captain puppet inside his sand bucket. He put in the sea shanty recording and his monkey's fist to show to Great Uncle Skipper Mouse. He added his treasure map, compass, and bosun's whistle. He tucked in a glove and baseball, and finally, in skinny spaces, he squeezed in a sand shovel and two favorite books.

Fribble snapped his suitcase shut and went to see how Scamper was doing. It was as bad as he had feared. Scamper's suitcase bulged way over the top.

"Will you help me squish it all in, Fribble?" he begged.

"There's no way all that is going to fit," Fribble told him. "Some things will have to be left." Fribble dumped everything out on the rug as Scamper sat back on his heels to watch.

"You've got five dump trucks in here and three shovels," Fribble said.

"But I need all my trucks and shovels for the beach," Scamper explained.

By eliminating a few things and squeezing others together, Fribble finally managed to close Scamper's suitcase. He half expected the lock to spring open, but it held.

They carried their suitcases downstairs and watched as Father packed them into the car. The backseat was already well supplied with water, healthy snacks, and a few travel toys.

Now that the car was packed, they all went back in the house and sat down to lunch. Afterwards, they cleared everything away and cleaned up the kitchen.

At last they were out the door, into the car, and heading through town to the highway. Father had marked the route they would follow with a yellow magic marker. He handed the map to Fribble and said, "I'm going to need you to help keep me on the right road, Fribble."

"I will," Fribble promised.

They drove through beautiful countryside from highway 41 to highway 43, and finally to highway 94. Their route took them right around the edge of Lake Michigan.

"Is that the Atlantic Ocean?" Scamper kept asking whenever he looked out the car window at the lake. "Are we there yet?"

The first night they stopped at the town of Kenosha. Fribble thought it was great fun to stop at a motel and share a big double bed with his little brother. That night, Fribble took the treasure map out of his suitcase and studied the clues again. He showed it to his father.

"What do you suppose these numbers are?" he asked. He pointed to numbers on a faint line that ran through the middle of the map that read 43.8366 and to numbers on a line that went from top to bottom on the map that read 65.5066. "Are they Dewey Decimal numbers like you find on books?"

"I don't think so," Father said. "I'm not sure, but I think those must be lines of latitude and longitude."

Fribble furrowed his brow trying to remember. "I think I've looked up places on a map in the big world atlas at school using latitude and longitude."

"You probably have," Father said.

"So maybe these numbers will tell us exactly where the 'X' is located," Fribble went on. "All we have to do is to look it up in an atlas."

"Hurrah!" Scamper shouted. "Then we'll know right where the treasure is." He paused. "Did you bring an atlas with you in your suitcase, Fribble?"

Fribble sighed. "No, Scamper. An atlas is a big heavy book filled with maps. I didn't bring one. We'd have to visit a library to find one."

"Is there a library in this town? Can we go tonight?" Scamper asked.

Mother said, "It's late. The library will be closed by now I'm afraid. But maybe we can stop at one in the next town tomorrow."

"And we have to get to bed," Father chimed in. "I want to get a really early start tomorrow and sneak through the Chicago area while traffic is light."

Next morning they were up early, and were soon traveling on highway 80. Scamper looked out the window and saw another great body of water.

"Is that the Atlantic Ocean?" he wanted to know.

"No, Scamper," Fribble said. He showed his little brother the road map. "You're looking at Lake Erie. We're still a long way from the ocean."

Mother wanted to enjoy every part of the trip, so they would often pull into a rest stop to stretch their legs or spend an hour at a picnic area. Sometimes they'd go into a restaurant along the way for something to eat or drink. The second night, they stayed in a motel in Ashtabula, Ohio.

As soon as they were in their motel room, Fribble asked, "Is there a library in this town? Can we go there and use an atlas?"

"You can look in the phone book and see," Mother suggested, "and find out how late they're open."

Fribble pulled a phone book out of a little chest of drawers by the bed and searched until he found the number of the Ashtabula Public Library. He phoned and found out where they were located and that they were open until 8:30 p.m.

After dinner, Fribble and his family drove to the Ashtabula Library. A friendly lady at the desk asked if she might help.

Fribble had written the number 43.8366 N and 69.5066 W on a piece of paper, because he didn't want to show his treasure map to just anyone. "I think these are latitude and longitude numbers," he said. "And I'm trying to find out where this spot is."

"You might look at a globe of the world," she suggested. "Once you find out where the place is, you may need a more detailed map to learn more."

The librarian showed them where a globe was located.

Fribble examined the globe carefully. He saw the tiny lines that went from the North Pole to the South Pole, and the imaginary line around the earth called the equator. There were numbers along these lines of latitude and longitude that divided the globe up into small sections. At 43 degrees north, and 69 degrees west, Fribble found himself pointing at the coast of Maine.

"Here it is!" he shouted, and then clamped a paw over his mouth. Remembering that he was in a library, he lowered his voice to a whisper, while his heart beat fast. "It's a spot in Maine." He looked at the tiny print and saw that the place where the lines crossed was right at the entrance of Johns Bay.

Fribble carefully wrote all this into his little spiral notebook.

It was almost time for the library to close, and they were all tired from their long day's drive. They quickly returned to the motel and crawled into bed. As Fribble fell asleep, thoughts of John Bay, the seashore, and pirate's treasure danced through his head.

Two days after they'd started their trip, in the middle of the afternoon, Fribble and his family drove up Bay Street in Edam, Maine, past rows of weathered wooden houses. Fribble had his nose pasted to the window looking for house number 1410.

"There it is!" Fribble shouted. "And look! It's dove gray, just like the clue in the treasure poem. I'll bet that map begins right here at Great Uncle Skipper's house!"

They pulled into the driveway and there was a mad scramble as everyone climbed out of the car at once. A tall figure, wearing a jaunty captain's hat, stepped out the door of the house onto the porch.

"Ahoy!" he called, "and welcome aboard."

It must be Great Uncle Skipper Mouse. Who else could it be?

"Hello, Skipper," Mother said. She reached him first and gave him a great big hug. Then Father enveloped him in another squeeze.

Great Uncle Skipper bent down and said, "Hello, there. You must be Scamper, the young artist who sent me such a beautiful sea picture." He offered his paw, and Scamper shook it and then, suddenly shy, ran to stand beside Mother.

While these greetings were going on, Fribble hung back just a little. His sharp eyes had taken in the big, old house that stood two stories high with its back facing the beach and the sea. Fribble's nose twitched as he sniffed the salty air.

"And you," Great Uncle Skipper said, standing straight with hands on hips and looking down at Fribble, "must be none other than Fribble, the Sailor Mouse."

"Aye, aye!" Fribble said, rushing forward to hug Great Uncle Skipper around the waist. "I've been waiting to see you!"

"I've been waiting, too!" Great Uncle Skipper said.

Great Uncle Skipper invited them all in and showed them to their rooms. Mother and Father had a big sunny upstairs room in the front of the house. Right next to them was a smaller room for

Scamper. And in back, with windows facing the sea, was Fribble's room, right next to Great Uncle Skipper's.

While Father brought in suitcases and deposited them in the various rooms, Great Uncle Skipper said, "You've had a long, hard drive. How about some tea and lemonade? And I've made a few cookies, too."

Mother helped make the tea and set out the cups and saucers. Great Uncle Skipper poured two tall glasses of lemonade for Fribble and Scamper and set them on the table with a plate of cookies. Fribble quickly nibbled one and found it very tasty indeed.

During much talking about the trip and the family, Fribble did his best to listen politely. Finally, when he couldn't bear to wait any longer, he said, "Please, please, could Scamper and I go down to the beach?"

"Of course," Great Uncle Skipper said. "It's right outside my back door. I'll go with you."

"While the rest of you go exploring, I'll get our things unpacked. Then a little later this evening, we want to take you out to dinner," Mother said, smiling at Great Uncle Skipper. "I don't want you to do a lot of cooking while we're here."

Father, Great Uncle Skipper, Scamper, and Fribble went out the door, down a short rocky path through the backyard, and found themselves right on the beach.

"Wow!" Fribble said. "You practically live in the ocean."

Scamper ran straight toward the water, stopping when he reached the wet sand. "Is this the Atlantic Ocean?" he asked.

"Yes, it is," Father said. "It's what you've been waiting for."

"Can we wade in?" Fribble begged.

"Yes, you may get your toes wet," Father agreed. "Take off your shoes and roll up your trousers. You can play for about an hour."

Fribble and Scamper had a great time sinking their toes into the sand and running away from the waves that came rushing up on the beach. Now and then, one of them would find a seashell and shout, "For Tweek," or "For Twitter," or "For me!"

They'd run from the water's edge back up to where Father and Great Uncle Skipper were talking, so that Father could keep the precious shells safe.

All too soon, it was time to return to Great Uncle Skipper's house, get cleaned up, and go out to eat.

They walked to a nearby restaurant and, after a dinner that included a delicious cream cheese dessert, they walked home again. Once they were all settled in chairs on the back porch facing the sea, Great Uncle Skipper said, "Now this next week, I want you folks to do whatever you'd like. We can make a plan and go somewhere every day, or we can sit on the porch, or stay on the beach and do nothing at all except build sand castles."

"I'd love to just sit and relax," Mother said, "and not drive anywhere."

"Me, too," Father agreed.

"I'm going to build a million sand castles," Scamper said.

"I want to do all that, too," Fribble said, "but not until after I find the treasure."

Great Uncle Skipper smiled. "So, you've been studying the treasure map, have you? What have you figured out so far?"

"Excuse me for just one minute," Fribble said. He raced back into the house and up to his room where he grabbed the treasure map. Then he ran back downstairs and out onto the porch.

He pointed to the little house. "I think this is your dove gray house, right here on Bay Street," he explained to Great Uncle Skipper. "And if it is, here's the road we have to take to get to the white sands. And see, this is the Atlantic," he pointed to the wavy lines, "so the spot we want is right on the ocean. I looked it up on a globe using those big longitude and latitude numbers. It showed that the spot marked 'X' is very near Johns Bay."

"My goodness," Great Uncle Skipper said. "You've almost got it figured out."

"What I need now," Fribble said, "is an atlas so that I can see exactly what's at that spot at Johns Bay."

"I just happen to have one," Great Uncle Skipper said. So Great Uncle Skipper went back inside with Fribble and Scamper to pore over the atlas.

Right next to Johns Bay was Muscongus Bay. Using the numbers he had written down, Fribble ran his paw along the lines of longitude and latitude on the atlas page to a little piece of land called Pemaquid Point at the edge of Johns Bay.

"That's it!" Fribble said. "Pemaquid Point. Could we drive down there tomorrow? Could we?"

"Let's see what your parents think," suggested Great Uncle Skipper.

"We'll get no peace until we finish this treasure hunt," Father said when asked about an outing to Pemaquid Point. "So we might as well go tomorrow."

"I'll make us a picnic," Mother promised.

That evening, Fribble showed off his sailor puppet to Great Uncle Skipper and told him how he could read the mariner's compass. He and Scamper tied sailor knots. Finally, Great Uncle Skipper joined them in singing "The Sailor's Alphabet," and then piped them to bed using the bosun's whistle.

The next morning, before they left the house, Mother went to her room and brought down a bag.

"I've got something for you," she said. "You can't hunt for treasure without wearing the right hat."

Mother reached inside and pulled out two pirate's hats that she had made for Scamper and Fribble. They were exactly like the fancy ones Fribble had found when he searched sailor hats on the Internet.

Fribble and Scamper squealed in glee as they pulled on their hats.

They all piled into the car, with Great Uncle Skipper sitting in back between the two handsome pirates. Using the treasure map he held in his paws, Fribble directed his father down one street and another, along the dotted route on the map toward Pemaquid Point. They reached a parking lot near the beach with picnic tables close by. Not far away stood several buildings, including a lighthouse.

"Look!" Fribble said when he scrambled out of the car. "It's just like the treasure map poem. White sand and ocean." He pulled the map out of his pocket and read:

> *"You start at a cottage, all grey like a gull,*
> *And make your way close by the sea*
> *Race over the white sand and remember that*
> *The map in your paws holds the key."*

"See? We've done all I just read." He went on reading.

"There on the spot, standing high on a cliff,
One eye winking very brightly."

Fribble interrupted himself to look around. "One eye?" he said, and frowned. Then a smile broke across his face. "It's the lighthouse. That is what is standing high on the cliff, and it's blinking toward the sea!"

Great Uncle Skipper said, "You're right Fribble. It blinks every six seconds."

Fribble continued reading,

"Climb up and up until you reach
Eleven and twenty-three."

Again Fribble stopped.

"Climb up and up what?" Scamper wanted to know.

"Steps!" Fribble shouted. "There must be steps in that lighthouse. That's what I'm supposed to climb. Come on, everybody. To the lighthouse!"

Everyone hurried over to the stone lighthouse and went inside. A volunteer near the door greeted them. "Hello, there!" he said. "Welcome. You must be the family that Skipper Mouse has been waiting for. Come on in. Skipper will be your guide."

Fribble read from his treasure map again. "Eleven and twenty-three," he said. "Let's see. That makes 34 steps we have to climb."

Fribble led the way to the first step and began counting as he went. "Thirty-one, thirty-two, thirty-three, thirty-four," coming to a halt on the thirty-fourth step.

He read the treasure map poem again, "Now look in the crack that's just to your left." Eagerly Fribble scanned the walls of the stone tower. At first he saw no cracks of any kind. Then near the foot of the stairs he thought he saw what looked like a little chink in the wall. Quickly, he bent down.

"What is it?" Scamper asked.

"I'm not sure," Fribble said. "But something." He scrabbled at the corner in the crack and gave a little tug. Out into his paws slid a silver coin. "Look!" he said standing up. "It's a quarter!"

"You found it! You found the treasure!" Scamper shouted.

"And it's not just any quarter," Fribble said, turning it over in his paws for a closer look. "There's a picture on one side of the Pemaquid Point lighthouse. Wow! What a treasure!"

He passed the quarter around so that everyone could admire it.

"That's what they chose to be on the Maine state quarter," Great Uncle Skipper Mouse said. "It's the symbol for our state."

"I'll never spend it," Fribble said. "I'm going to save this and my treasure map forever and ever." He hugged Great Uncle Skipper.

They continued up the stairs to see the huge lens that flashed a warning out to sailors at sea who might be lost and too close to the rocks during fog or a storm. From the top they stared at the granite cliff dropping from the lighthouse to the sea. After they climbed down, they stopped in the gift shop where Great Uncle Skipper bought the boys a book telling the history of the stone lighthouse and the keepers of the light.

After their picnic lunch, they all drove back to Great Uncle Skipper's house.

"No doubt about it!" Great Uncle Skipper said, as they climbed out of the car and headed inside. "I know sailor mice when I see them. The two of you are bound to love the sea. I'm so glad you're all spending your vacation here. Now, let's all put on our swimsuits, explore the ocean, and find more treasures on the beach!"

As Fribble and Scamper raced to their rooms to change into their swimsuits, Scamper said. "Isn't it great that the map led you right to the silver quarter in the lighthouse?"

"Yes," Fribble agreed, "figuring out every one of the secrets in the sea chest has been fun, but best of all, that map led us right here to Edam, Maine, where we discovered that Great Uncle Skipper Mouse is the best treasure of all!"